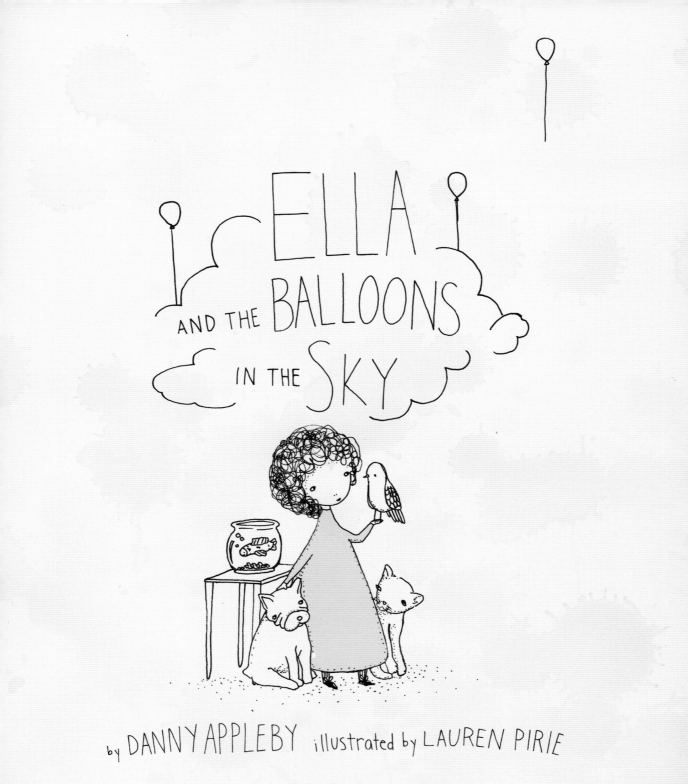

ELLA AND THE BALLOONS IN THE SKY

by DANNY APPLEBY   illustrated by LAUREN PIRIE

Tundra Books
www.tundrabooks.com

Published in Canada by Tundra Books, a division of Random House of Canada Limited,
One Toronto Street, Suite 300, Toronto, Ontario M5C 2V6

Published in the United States by Tundra Books of Northern New York,
P.O. Box 1030, Plattsburgh, New York 12901

Library of Congress Control Number: 2012955582

LIBRARY AND ARCHIVES CANADA CATALOGUING IN PUBLICATION

Appleby, Danny
Ella and the balloons in the sky / by Danny Appleby ;
illustrated by Lauren Pirie.

ISBN 978-1-77049-528-9. – ISBN 978-1-77049-529-6 (EPUB)

I. Pirie, Lauren II. Title.

PS8601.P63E55 2013   jC813'.6   C2012-908438-7

We acknowledge the financial support of the Government of Canada through
the Canada Book Fund and that of the Government of Ontario through the Ontario
Media Development Corporation's Ontario Book Initiative. We further acknowledge
the support of the Canada Council for the Arts and the Ontario Arts Council
for our publishing program.

ONTARIO ARTS COUNCIL
CONSEIL DES ARTS DE L'ONTARIO

Edited by Samantha Swenson
Designed by Lauren Pirie
The artwork in this book was rendered in ink and tea on paper.
This book is set in Providence Sans

www.tundrabooks.com

Printed and bound in China

1 2 3 4 5 6   18 17 16 15 14 13

for Ella

♡

Three days
before
Ella
turned nine,
a most
peculiar thing
she did find.

In the morning
when she went
to feed
all her pets,
her dog,
fish,
bird,
cat,
and
all of
the rest,

there

was

no dog in its house,

no fish in its bowl,

no bird in its cage,

and no cat at all.

"Where are you?"
she asked.
"Where have you gone?"

She searched
the
whole
house

and even the lawn.

Then from the sky
she heard some
faint sounds,

like a bark

and a chirp

and a splash

and

M E O W

There up in the clouds,
afloat overhead,
they were tied to balloons,
blue   green
yellow   and red

"Come down!"
Ella cried.
"Come down
and stay!"

But they rose
higher and higher
and farther away.

So she
climbed to the
top of the
tallest of trees,
and she
reached
and she
stretched
as far as
could be.

But the strings
were too far,
the balloons
were too high,
the cat's tail
was too short,
and her dog
waved good-bye.

And
Mom
said...

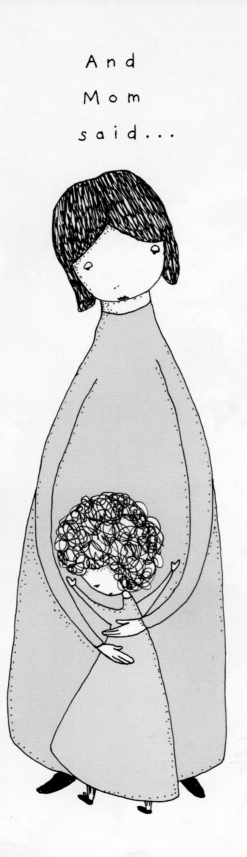

When things float away
we must stay on the ground
and know in our hearts that
someday they'll be found.

But Ella reached to the ground
for the sharpest sharp rock,
and she threw it up high,
and expected a "pop!"

But as hard as she threw,
as hard as she tried,
her rock couldn't touch
those balloons in the sky.

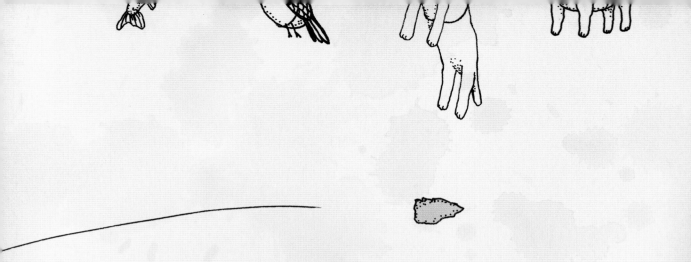

And
again
Mom
said...

When things float away
we must stay on the ground
and know in our hearts that
someday they'll be found.

Ella thought long and hard

until she got such a hunch,

she took a hundred balloons

that she tied in a bunch.

And she ran and she jumped

and she twirled and she leaped,

but those balloons

wouldn't lift up

her nine-

(in three days)

year-old-feet.

"Mom!"
Ella cried.
"They're floating away!
I love them so much,
I want them to stay!"

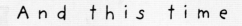

And this time
Mom said...

When things float away
you must say good-bye,
but when you miss them the most,
just look up to the sky.

And so Ella decided
to listen to Mom.
She stopped trying to fly
and she sat on the lawn.

She remembered her pets
and their little pet faces
and saw magical things
in some everyday places,
like her bird in a cloud
and her dog in a tree,
with his eyes in the trunk
and his ears in the leaves.

Like the face of her cat
in the sun's shiny rays
with the faintest "meow"
on the sunniest days.

And when those days
turned to nights
and her pets seemed so far,
Ella looked to the sky
and saw her fish in the stars.

It was then that she knew
it wasn't good-bye,
that her friends weren't lost
up there in the sky.

They'd just
floated to
somewhere she
hadn't yet been, to magical
places she hadn't yet seen.

As long as

she knew

they could

always be found,

they'd stay

in her heart

right here on

the ground.